# The Night I Was Chased by a Vampire

"Umansky sustains our interest, and a consistently excellent level of writing, right to the poem's fine (and suprising) conclusion."

*The Independent*

"I read this to 115 Year 5's at an end of term assembly and they were so keen I had to read it twice. Powerful stuff indeed."

*Books for Keeps*

"Children who like vampires and funny, spooky tales will love it."

*Times Educational Supplement*

*Also by Kaye Umansky and Keren Ludlow*

The Empty Suit of Armour
The Bogey Men and the Trolls Next Door
The Spooks Step Out

# The Night I Was Chased by a Vampire

## KAYE UMANSKY

### Illustrated by Keren Ludlow

A Dolphin
Paperback

Published in paperback in 1996

This edition published in 2006 for Index Books Limited

First published in Great Britain in 1995
by Orion Children's Books
a division of the Orion Publishing Group Ltd
Orion House
5 Upper St Martin's Lane
London WC2H 9EA

A catalogue record for this book is available
from the British Library

Printed in Great Britain by Clays Ltd, St Ives plc

ISBN 1 85881 251 8

I was walking one night in the mountains,

My fingers were blue with the frost.

I stood in the snow.

I thought, "Where shall I go?"

It was late. It was cold. I was lost.

I wasn't quite sure how I got there.
I'd been to my aunty's for tea.
But my sense of direction was faulty
And I took a wrong turn. (Silly me.)

The forest was dark as a dungeon.

I couldn't stay there, or I'd freeze.

I couldn't just stand

With my head in my hand

And the snow coming up to my knees . . .

But how to get out

Was a matter for doubt.

Straight ahead?

    Up or down?

        Left or right?

I couldn't decide.

Then I suddenly spied

Through the trees, in the distance

    – A LIGHT!

It came from a tumbledown castle
With turrets and towers and spires,
I hurried right up,
Thinking "Soup in a cup!
Warm water! Thick blankets! Hot fires!"

The castle was smothered with ivy.

There was moss on each crumbling wall.

It was, I suspected,

Quite badly neglected.

Not what I'd expected at all.

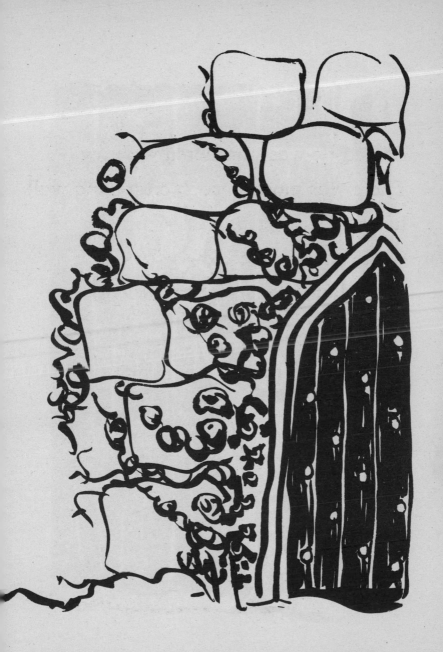

But with knocker in hand

I took a bold stand

And I called, in a confident way,

"Open up! Here's a lost, lonely traveller,

Who's looking for somewhere to stay!"

From within, there came shuffling footsteps.
The door slowly opened a crack.
"Well, hello there," I said.
"Any chance of a bed?
And a bath? And a bit of a snack?"

I suppose you would call him a butler.
(Though no other butler I've seen
Was built like a sack of potatoes
With eyes quite so piggy and mean.)

He was badly in need of a haircut.

It hung to his shoulders like rope,

Not to mention a scrub

In a scalding hot tub

With a broom and a big bar of soap.

He stared in surprise
With his little pig eyes
Then he scratched his great stomach,
and laughed.
Then he gave a sly grin
And said, "Come right on in."
So I did. I went in.
(Which was daft.)

The hallway was shrouded in shadow.
Dark tapestries reached to the ground,
Cold faces stared out from old paintings.
Their eyes seemed to follow me round.

The biggest hung over the fireplace,
I paused for a moment beneath.
This painting was not like the others.
It followed me round with its teeth!

"Who's that?" I enquired of the butler,

"That chap with the fangs in his face?"

He hissed, " 'tis the master!"

And hobbled off faster.

And I had to run to keep pace.

"So tell me, my man," I persisted,
"This master of yours. Is he here?
Does he stay out of sight?
Will I meet him tonight?"
"Well, you might," he replied with a leer

Through corridors, narrow and winding

We hastened, in deepening gloom.

Then he set down his candle,

Took hold of a handle,

And said, "This is it. Here's your room."

The bedroom was most uninviting,
The cobwebs were thick overhead.
There were shadows that capered in corners
And a saggy old four-poster bed.

"It's charming!" I cried,

(Well, all right, so I lied,

But there's no harm in being polite.)

He gave a brief shrug,

Gave his forelock a tug,

Then he grunted and wished me goodnight.

But the night wasn't good. No, it wasn't.
The blankets smelled badly of mould
And I needed to visit the bathroom.
(I told you before, it was *cold*.)

By the flickering light of a candle,
I hastily rose and got dressed,
And I stealthily slipped from my bedroom,
And boldly set forth on my quest.

I walked down the echoing passage
Not knowing which way I should go.
Then I came to a crumbling stairway
Which plunged into darkness below.

I followed it down to a dungeon.

(I shouldn't have done, but I did.)

And there – shock of shocks!

I discovered a box –

Yes, a long wooden box with a lid!

Then the lid of that box began rising!

I let out a horrified shout.

I went cold, I went hot,

I was stuck to the spot . . .

. . . *As the man called The Master stepped out.*

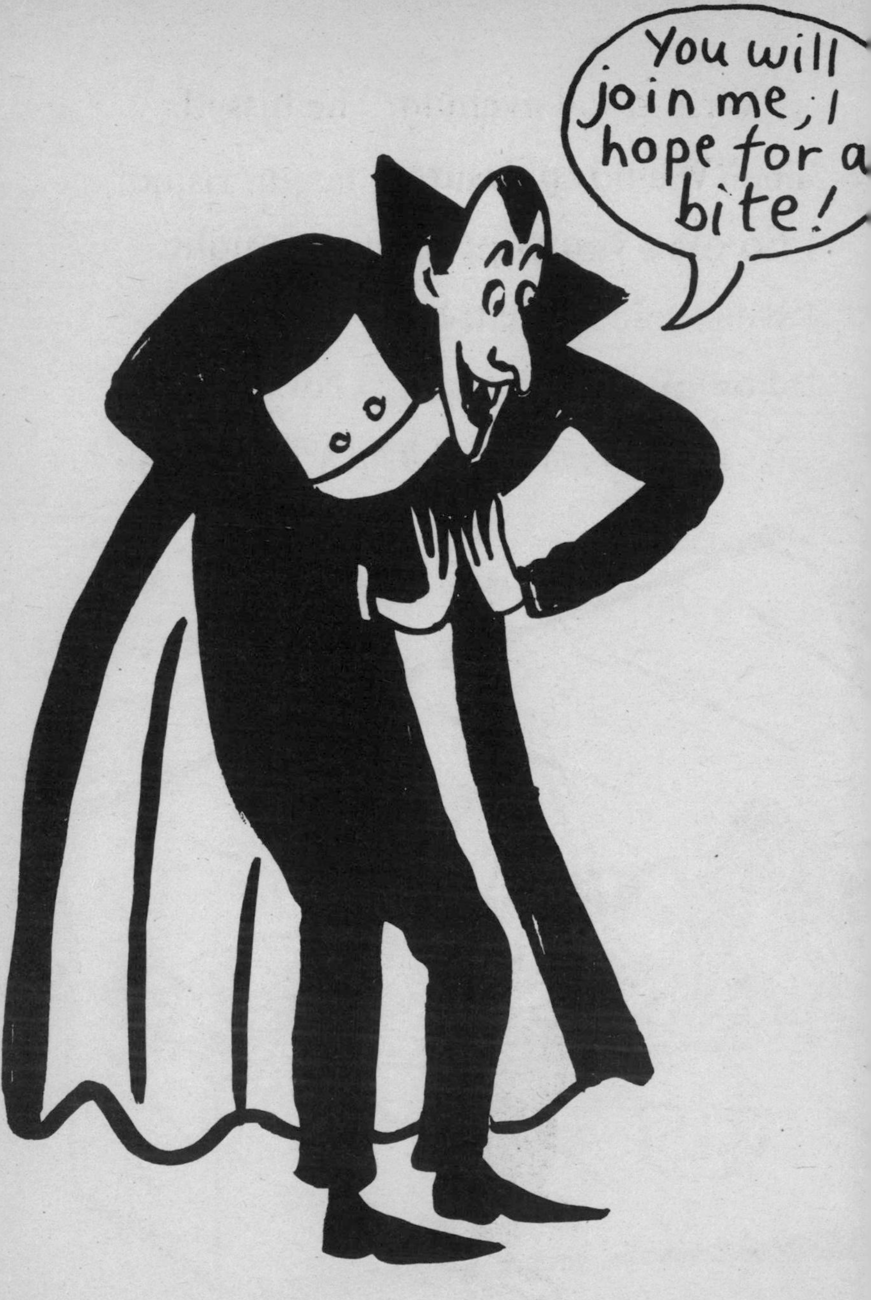
You will join me, I hope for a bite!

"Well, good evening," he hissed.

"What a pleasure.

So glad you popped over tonight.

It is such a rare treat

To have folks round to eat.

You will join me, I hope, for a bite?"

I did not like the way that he said it.
I did not like the gleam in his eyes.
So I did the one thing I could think of.
I turned and I ran. (Which was wise.)

I raced up the twisting old stairway
With the speed of a runaway horse.
From behind came the voice of the master:
"Hey, you! Come on back!

    *You're first course!*"

I raced through the crumbling castle.
The master was hot on my heels,
Insisting I join him for dinner.
I ignored his pathetic appeals.

He chased me down stairs and
    through hallways,
He chased me up high and down low,
In the whole of that crumbling castle
There was nowhere that we didn't go.

I did what I could to outrun him,
In fact, I was gaining a bit –
Then I turned a sharp bend
And I reached a dead end.
There was nowhere to go. This was IT.

I was trapped like a rat in a corner
I had to escape him – but how?
I had no time to beg,
He caught hold of my leg
Which he p–u–l–l–e–d. . .

LIKE I'M PULLING YOURS NOW!